Katie and the Sunflowers

James Mayhew

KT-153-693

ORCHARD BOOKS

For Margaret
and all the children and staff at
Tacolneston Primary School, Norfolk,
~ with love and admiration ~
And for Sue, who likes sunflowers,
~ with love ~

Orchard Books
96 Leonard Street, London EC2A 4XD
Orchard Books Australia
Unit 31/56 O'Riordan Street, Alexandria, NSW 2015
1 86039 989 4 (hardback)
1 84121 634 8 (paperback)
First published in Great Britain in 2000
First paperback publication in 2001
Copyright © James Mayhew 2000
The right of James Mayhew to be identified as
the author and illustrator of this work has been asserted
by him in accordance with the Copyright,
Designs and Patents Act, 1988.
A CIP catalogue record for this book is available
from the British Library.
1 2 3 4 5 6 7 8 9 10 (hardback)
6 7 8 9 10 (paperback)
Printed in Belgium

Grandma was helping Katie plant some seeds
in the garden when it started to rain.

"Never mind," said Grandma. "The rain
will make everything grow."

"But what shall we do now?" said Katie.

"Let's go to the gallery," said Grandma.
"You always have fun there."

When they arrived, Grandma sat down to rest, so
Katie went off by herself to look around.
The gallery was full of warm sunny paintings. Katie
liked a painting called *Sunflowers* by Vincent Van Gogh.

The sunflowers looked dry and crunchy and were full of seeds.

"Perhaps I could grow the seeds in my garden," said Katie. She slowly reached out and found she could touch them!

But Katie knocked the vase. It wobbled and fell right out of the picture, spilling sunflowers and seeds all over the floor.

"Oh no," said Katie. "I'd better clear this up before anyone sees."

Just then Katie heard someone laughing. She looked around but there was no one else in the room. The laughter was coming from a painting called *Breton Girls Dancing* by Paul Gauguin.

"What's so funny?" said Katie, climbing inside.

Katie saw that she was beside a
farm. The girls, who were called Masie,
Musette and Mimi, giggled and
pointed to the mess in the gallery.

"You'll be in trouble if anyone
finds out," Mimi said.

"Well, I didn't mean to knock over
the vase," said Katie. "I don't suppose
you could help me clear it all up?"

"We're too tired," said Masie.

"We've been dancing all day," said Musette.

"What about you?" said Katie to Mimi.

"Only if I can bring Zazou," said Mimi,
picking up her dog.

"I suppose it's all right," said Katie. "Let's go."

So they went through the
frame and into the gallery.

Mimi and Katie gathered up the sunflowers, but
Zazou wanted to play. He snatched the sunflowers
away in his mouth and ran off with them.

"How can we put the picture back together
now?" said Katie crossly.

"I'm sorry, *mon amie*," said Mimi. "Let's try
to catch him!"

They chased Zazou but he was too quick for them. He suddenly took a flying leap towards a painting called *Café Terrace at Night* by Vincent Van Gogh and disappeared inside.

Katie and Mimi jumped in after him.

Zazou refused to let go
of the sunflowers.
He darted in and out
of the tables and chairs,
knocking plates and
cups flying.

Then Zazou ran between the waiter's legs.
"*Zut alors!*" said the waiter, dropping a plate of iced
cakes. He was very angry. He chased Katie, Mimi and
Zazou right through the frame and back into the gallery.

"What are we going to do?" panted Mimi.

"I've got an idea," said Katie, pointing to a painting by Paul Cézanne. It was called *Still Life, with Apples and Oranges.* "Come on, I need your help!"

Katie put her hand into the painting and grabbed one end of a cloth. She told Mimi to hold the other end.

"Now pull!" yelled Katie.

The bowls of fruit tipped up and apples and oranges came tumbling into the gallery, just as the waiter caught up with them.

He slipped on the fruit and spun around
till he was dizzy.

"*Zut alors!*" he yelled.

"I wonder where Zazou went," said Mimi.

"He must be here somewhere," said Katie,
as they dashed away.

"*Hélas!*" said Mimi. "I shall never find him and he'll be lost in the gallery for ever."

"Nonsense," said Katie. "I can hear a dog barking."

They followed the noise and there at the end of the corridor was Zazou.

He had dropped the sunflowers and was barking at a bright red dog in a painting called *Tahitian Pastorals* by Paul Gauguin. The other dog barked back and Zazou jumped inside the picture.

"Your dog is nothing but trouble," said Katie as they clambered after him.

Zazou and the red dog
barked at one another, wagging their tails.
    "Welcome to our island!" said two
beautiful women.
    It was very peaceful, full of scented
lilies and blossom, with the sea lapping
on the beach.
        "Phew!" said Katie. "It's very hot
        here. Let's go for a paddle."

While Zazou and the red dog ran about on the
sand, Katie and Mimi splashed around in the sea.
Zazou was busy digging a hole when, all of a
sudden, he disappeared.

"Where has he gone?" said Mimi.
Katie looked into the hole. It was
very large. Right at the bottom she
saw Zazou sitting on top of a big
chest. Mimi and Katie slowly opened
the lid. It was full of gold coins!

"Pirate treasure!" said Katie,
showing the women. "What
will you do with it?"

"We don't use money on our island, we have everything
we need," they said. "You can have it if you want!"

Katie took a handful of coins and thanked the women.
Then she, Mimi and Zazou went through the frame
and back into the gallery.

Katie quickly picked up the sunflowers before Zazou
could grab them again.

"We'd better put these back," she said. "Which way is it?"

"I'm not sure, *mon amie*," said Mimi. "I think we're lost!"

Then they saw Zazou sniffing at something on the ground.

"Sunflower seeds!" said Katie. "Zazou's left a trail of them.
What a clever dog, I'm glad he came after all!"

Mimi gathered Zazou up in
her arms and they followed
the trail of sunflower seeds
back to the Cézanne still life.

They carefully put all
the fruit back and then
went on to the café
picture by Van Gogh.

The waiter was standing there with a piece of paper in his hand.

"It's a bill," said Mimi. "For the cakes and everything."

Katie dug into her pocket and took out the gold coins.

"Is this enough?" she said to the waiter.

"*Merci!*" he said, looking very pleased. "You may eat cakes here whenever you want!" and he climbed back into his picture.

Then Katie and Mimi followed the seeds back to the sunflower picture. Katie collected a few seeds and wrapped them in her hankie and put them in her coat pocket. Then she carefully put the sunflowers back.

"Almost as good as new!" said Katie. "Thanks for coming with me."

"I'm glad I did, *mon amie*," said Mimi. "It was fun!" and she hopped into her picture with Zazou.

Katie ran off to find her Grandma, who was just waking up.

"Shall we see if it's stopped raining?" Grandma said.

It hadn't, but Katie didn't mind. "Rain is good for the garden," she said. "It will make everything grow."

The Post-Impressionists

Vincent Van Gogh, Paul Gauguin and Paul Cézanne followed the Impressionists, and so were called the Post-Impressionists. Like the Impressionists they used bright colours and thick paint, but they used colours and brushstrokes in a different way, painting pictures that showed their feelings and moods.

Vincent Van Gogh (1853-1890)

Vincent Van Gogh is famous for his use of colour, which makes his paintings look almost alive. The paint is very thick and the colour is very bright. The *Sunflowers* is a good example of this. You can see it in the National Gallery, London, England. He also painted the *Café Terrace at Night*, in Arles, France, where he lived for a while. It is now in the Kröller-Muller Museum, in Holland where Van Gogh was born.

When Van Gogh was alive, not many people liked his paintings because they were so different from anything they had seen before.

Paul Gauguin (1848-1903)

Paul Gauguin was born in France. He liked Van Gogh's paintings and they worked together for a while. They even painted pictures of each other. Gauguin painted *Breton Girls Dancing* around this time. It's now in the National Gallery of Art in Washington DC. Later Gauguin moved to Tahiti where the tropical colours inspired him to paint in an exciting new way. *Tahitian Pastorals*, which is now in the Hermitage Museum, St Petersburg, Russia, is typical of this style. Gauguin had some sunflower seeds sent to Tahiti because sunflowers didn't grow there. Perhaps he wanted them to remind him of France and his old friend Van Gogh.

Paul Cézanne (1839-1906)

Paul Cézanne was also born in France. He knew both Van Gogh and Gauguin. He arranged colours and shapes very carefully and the more he painted, the more abstract his pictures became. It took him a long time to paint a picture. If he painted people they had to sit still for many days, so it was easier to paint still-lifes and landscapes. His last paintings influenced so many artists that he is called 'the father of modern art'. You can see *Still Life, with Apples and Oranges* at the Musée d'Orsay in Paris, France.

Paintings by these three artists can be found in museums and galleries all over the world.

Acknowledgements

Sunflowers by Vincent Van Gogh © National Gallery, London. Breton Girls Dancing, Pont-Aven, 1888 by Paul Gauguin, Richard Carafelli; © Board of Trustees, National Gallery of Art, Washington DC. Café Terrace at Night, 'Place du Forum', Arles, 1888 by Vincent Van Gogh Kröller-Muller Museum, The Netherlands. Still Life, with Apples and Oranges, 1895-1900 (oil on canvas) by Paul Cézanne (1839-1906) Musée d'Orsay, Paris, France/Peter Willi/Bridgeman Art Library. Tahitian Pastorals, 1893 by Paul Gauguin (1848-1903) Hermitage, St Petersburg, Russia/Bridgeman Art Library.